Callie and The Stepmother

Susan A. Meyers

Callie and the Stepmother

Blooming Tree Press
P.O. Box 140934
Austin, Texas 78714-0934
Copyright © 2005 by Susan A. Meyers
Cover art and interior illustrations by Rose Gauss
Cover design by Kelly Bell
Book design by Kelly Bell
Logo by Tabi Designs
Editor - Judy Gregerson
Copy editing by Peggy Brandt
Library of Congress Catalog Card Number: 2005921752
ISBN: 0-9718348-0-6
www.bloomingtreepress.com

Blooming Tree Press
P.O. Box 140934
Austin, Texas, 78714-0934

Printed in the United States of America

Dedication

Callie and the Stepmother is dedicated to a
lot of people who have believed in me.
To my husband, son, and family for whom it
was never "if" I got published, but "when."
To my critique groups, both online and
local, who put a lot of time and effort into
making Callie the best book it could be.
To God, who gave me the desire and talent to write.
And to all the wonderful people at Blooming Tree
Press who have made this such a wonderful experience.
Thanks so much for the encouragement, support
and love. Both "Callie" and I thank you!

God bless,
Susan

Contents

Illustrations

1

Callie

Callie's new stepmother, Pam, only pretended to be nice. But Callie wasn't fooled. She knew she was only waiting. Just like a spider waits in its web.

And now Callie's dad was leaving.

He hugged her hard against his soft, flannel shirt. His light beard scratched her cheek as she hugged him back.

"Daddy, can't I go with you?"

He touched her nose with his finger. "I'm sorry, princess, but the rules say nobody rides in my truck but me. You'll have fun with Pam. And this will give you some time to get to know her."

Callie wanted to grab his legs.

She wanted to beg him not to go.

Instead, she watched him pick up his suitcase. When he waved goodbye, she waved back. She wanted to shout, "Don't leave me with an evil stepmother." But she didn't.

Everyone knew how mean stepmothers were when the real dads went away. Then the stepmother's smile would turn to a snarl. She would be cruel. Just like in Cinderella.

But if Callie tried to explain, her dad would just shake his head. He'd say she'd been reading too many fairy tales.

As Dad drove away, her stepmother, Pam, laid a hand on her shoulder. "Sweetie, even though your dad's going to be gone for a couple of days, I want you to feel at home here."

But Callie knew better. Head hanging, she started toward the doorway to her new bedroom. Her fourteen-year-old stepsister stood in the way. Arms crossed and chin stuck out, she glared first at her mother and then at Callie.

"Well, I cleaned out one side of my closet and two drawers." Andrea said. "But I still don't want to share my room with a baby."

I'm not a baby, Callie wanted to say. But she didn't. What if they sent her to the attic to sleep? No matter what the fairy tales said, she didn't really believe any mice would help her. Turning, she saw that her stepmother had followed her down the hallway. She caught what looked like an evil scowl cross her face. Callie bit her bottom lip. If Pam sent her to the attic, she wouldn't give them the satisfaction of seeing her cry.

But all her stepmother said was, "Andrea, be nice to Callie. This is her home now, too."

Andrea rolled her eyes and sighed. Then she turned and went back into the bedroom.

Pam patted Callie on the shoulder. "It'll be okay. She's never had to share a room before. And Callie, I'm always here if you need to talk." She went back down the hall towards the kitchen.

Callie stood alone in the hallway. In the sudden silence, her breathing sounded loud in her ears. Not daring to go into the room, she slid against the wall until she sat on the floor.

Why had her stepmother been nice to her and not Andrea?

2

The Nightmare

*t*hat night Callie had a nightmare. As she scrubbed the fireplace, soot and ashes floated around her. Some of them fell on her thin blond hair. Some of them clung to her faintly pink cheeks. Instead of jeans and a tee shirt she wore an old patched gray dress. It had holes under the elbows. The harder she scrubbed, the dirtier the fireplace seemed to get.

Standing behind her, the frowning stepmother shouted, "Cleaner! Cleaner!" Callie's hands shook so hard she almost dropped the scrub brush. Two big fat tears started down her cheeks.

Callie woke up. She tried to take a big sniff, but her nose was all clogged up. She'd been crying in her sleep and now her eyes felt all sore and puffy. She rubbed them, wishing she dared get up and find a tissue. Instead, she took the end of her pillowcase and wiped them dry.

Stepdaughters always had to clean fireplaces. Soon she'd be cleaning the one in Pam's family room. She just knew it!

If only she could hold out until her dad came home. He'd be home in three more days! Then he'd make everything all right.

But even as she thought it, Callie shook her head. Would her dad really be able to change anything? Cinderella's dad had never been able to stop the wicked stepmother. Snow White's dad had never been able to help her.

No! Evil stepmothers were just too powerful.

Callie and the Stepmother

3
The Fireplace

*t*he next morning, Callie and Andrea sat eating breakfast. Matt, Callie's new stepbrother, also sat at the table.

"Callie." Her stepmother smiled, "I know you miss your dad." She reached over and patted her hand. "But he promised to call tomorrow. That's something fun to look forward to, isn't it?"

"Yes, ma'am."

Her stepmother frowned. "Don't you think we can find something else for you to call me besides ma'am? Pam would be okay if you're comfortable with that."

"Okay."

No way she'd think about it! In fairy tales the stepmother never had a name. Friends called each other by names, and her stepmother was *not* her friend.

"Just be careful in *my* room," Andrea told her. She threw her napkin down beside her bowl and leaned towards Callie. "I've got a lot of stuff that can get broken. Also, don't go touching any more of my things. My shampoo wasn't where I left it. You didn't use any of it, did you?" She leaned back in her chair, arms folded.

Unfair!

"I'm not a baby," Callie told her. With her balled fists, she squeezed so hard that she could feel her fingernails biting into her palms. "I know how to take care of stuff. And the only reason I moved your shampoo is because it kept falling into the bathtub while I was taking a bath."

"That sounds reasonable to me," said Pam. She put an arm around the back of her daughter's chair. "Doesn't it to *you*, Andrea Jane?"

Andrea shrugged. "Whatever." And that seemed to be the end of it, at least for her.

Callie's stomach felt as if a hundred super balls bounced around inside of it. Again, her stepmother had taken her side over Andrea's.

"The fireplace needs cleaning," her stepmother announced.

Silence. The balls in Callie's stomach bounced harder.

"I said," she repeated, "the fireplace needs cleaning."

Slowly Callie pushed back her chair. Her eyes blinked in rapid motion as she tried to keep tears from falling. Her heart pounded. She hadn't even finished her breakfast. She wondered if she dared ask where they kept the scrub brush?

"Callie, sweetie," Pam said, "your eggs'll get cold if you don't eat them now." She turned to her silent son. "Matt, did you hear me?"

"But I'm meeting my friends," twelve-year-old Matt protested.

"You mean," Callie's voice squeaked out, "Matt has to clean out the fireplace?"

Her stepmother looked surprised. "Of course he does, Callie. It's one of his chores." She smiled. "Sweetie, I wouldn't make you do such a big chore."

Callie looked down at her plate. She took a deep breath and then another, trying to get her heart to slow down. Everyone knew the stepchild had to do all the work. What was this stepmother up to?

4
Another Nightmare

*t*his time in Callie's nightmare, her stepmother held out a huge bowl of apples.
There were small apples and large apples, green
apples, and red. They all looked plump and
delicious. But one of them had lots of poison
in it. Callie didn't know how she knew that,
but she did.

Her stepmother grinned wickedly.
"Callie, I bought these just for you."

Tiny pricks of fear began going up and down Callie's back. Her stepmother would get mad if she didn't eat one. She stretched out her shaking hand over the pile of apples. Even if she didn't get the poisoned one, the stepmother would make her eat each and every apple until she did. Would the poison be in the biggest one or the smallest? Her hand closed over a bright Golden Delicious...

With a startle, Callie woke up. Andrea mumbled in her sleep, but didn't wake. Callie's heart beat wildly. She brushed at bangs made wet by sweat and then pulled the covers up until they came to her chin.

Would her stepmother really try to poison her?

Callie and the Stepmother

5

Poisoned?

*t*he next evening, the neighbors across the
street invited Matt, Andrea, and Callie to
go out for pizza. Matt and Andrea went. But
Callie had to stay home.

Her stepmother acted caring. "I'm sorry,
Callie, but I think you're coming down with a
cold. It's probably better if you stay home and
get some rest."

Callie wasn't getting a cold. She'd only
sneezed five times during morning church. But

why protest? Stepchildren weren't allowed to have fun. She clamped her lips together. She wanted to cry so bad that it hurt to breathe. But she wouldn't. Her stepmother would never know how sad she felt. Nope, Callie wouldn't give her the satisfaction.

But tears threatened to fall when she saw her dinner. Instead of hot, gooey, cheesy pizza, Callie got broccoli and cheese casserole.

"With a little chicken and rice thrown in," her stepmother said cheerfully. "Matt and Andrea love it. I hope you will too."

Visions of Snow White and the poisoned apple flew through Callie's head. Not that she really thought her stepmother would try to poison her. Instead, the food would *taste* like poison.

That's why cleaning the fireplace hadn't been her job. And why she hadn't been put in the attic to sleep. Snow White's stepmother had used an old woman's disguise to fool Snow White. But this stepmother used kindness. It made the broccoli and cheese casserole even meaner.

Her stepmother frowned at her. She touched Callie's forehead as if checking for a fever. "Aren't you hungry?"

Callie knew she had to eat. She couldn't let her stepmother see she'd figured out her evil plan. Slowly, Callie took a forkful of the casserole. Maybe she could wash it down quickly with a big swallow of milk?

Callie's eyes widened in surprise. The casserole wasn't horrible tasting. In fact, it tasted good. So good that she had two helpings.

"Callie? Would you like to hear a joke?" asked Pam from across the table.

Surprised, Callie nodded. For the first time since her father had left, she realized most of the knots in her stomach were gone.

"What building has the most stories?"

Callie shook her head.

"The library!"

Callie found herself laughing.

But stepmothers weren't supposed to know jokes. What was she up to now?

6

Lost!

*t*hat evening, Callie's father called. "How's my little princess?"

Callie wanted to cry. She wanted to tell him to come and get her.

But would he believe her if she said her stepmother was wicked? And what would happen if her stepmother found out Callie knew she was evil? It was better to say nothing.

"I love you, Daddy."

"I love you too, princess. Be good."

"I will." She took a deep breath. "Daddy, could you come home early?" Biting her lip, she crossed her fingers, hoping the wish would come true.

"What's wrong, sweetie? Pam said you might be getting a cold. If you need anything, I know she'll help you."

Her stepmother had already fooled her dad with the cold story. If Callie complained, her dad would just think it was because she wasn't feeling well. "No, I'm feeling better. I just miss you," she said. *I need you to come and save me*, she thought.

"Me too, princess. I'll see you tomorrow."

The next morning Pam asked Callie to help her. "I want to bake a cake for Matt's birthday. But I'm out of eggs. Would you mind going to the corner store for me? I'd ask Andrea or Matt, but they're both at ball practice."

Now Callie understood. Fetching and carrying were to be her life. Just like Cinderella. She also bet she wouldn't get a cake on her birthday. Not only that, but there most certainly wouldn't be any presents. In fact, her stepmother would probably demand that no one even mention Callie's birthday!

She hardly listened as the stepmother gave her careful directions to the store. Instead, she wondered if she would be allowed to eat any of the cake. Probably not. They'd all be sitting around the table, eating. She would be standing behind the stepmother's chair, waiting on them. Yeah, that was it. She would be the servant. If she were lucky, she'd get to lick the bowl when she washed it.

Callie took her time walking. First, she stopped and smelled some pretty red flowers. They weren't Andrea's, so her stepsister couldn't yell at her for sniffing them. Then she peeked in a bakery window. No cakes in there belonged to her stepmother, so she couldn't tell her not to look at them. After that, she patted a dog on a leash.

At least she got to go outside. She wasn't
locked in an attic where she had to mend
clothes all day long.

Callie turned left at the corner. This
way had a brick sidewalk. She skipped along,
counting the bricks as she went. Suddenly she
looked up. She saw lots of traffic. That wasn't
right. Her stepmother had said she wouldn't
have to cross any big streets. Slowly, Callie
started back the way she had come. She must
have missed the turn while counting bricks.
But she couldn't find any street like the one
her stepmother had described.

Callie started to get scared. She turned
one way and then another. Biting her lip, she
tried to keep from panicking. Still, a cold chill

ran up her spine. It was just like Hansel and Gretel. Only instead of getting lost in the woods, she had gotten lost in the city. And she hadn't thought about dropping bread crumbs so she could find her way back.

She choked back tears as she realized the stepmother had won. She'd gotten rid of Callie.

"Where is Callie?" Her dad would ask.

And the stepmother would pretend to cry. She'd hide her face in a tissue so he wouldn't see that she was really laughing. "Oh, I'm so sorry," she'd say, "but Callie got lost."

And would her dad care? After all, he had a new daughter now. Her stepsister would be happy that she didn't have to share a room.

No one would miss Callie, no one at all.

7
Saved!

*t*wo big tears trickled down Callie's cheeks. She imagined herself dressed in rags. She would have to search through garbage cans hoping for some small morsel to eat. What if she froze to death when it snowed? Would her stepmother be sorry?

Then she heard what sounded like her name.

"Callie!"

She turned and saw a woman hurrying toward her. The woman's pale face looked tight with worry. It was her stepmother. Callie was so relieved to be found that she forgot to be scared. She didn't care what the stepmother did to her, as long as she took her home.

As she reached Callie, she took hold of both her shoulders. She gently squeezed them. "Oh, sweetie, I'm so glad I found you. I'm so sorry, Callie. I just…well, Andrea and Matt are so much older…I should never have sent you to the store alone."

Astonished, Callie stared into her stepmother's face. "You really came here just to find me?"

"Why of course I did, honey. You're very important to me."

And Callie believed her.

They walked hand in hand the right way to the store. Callie smiled shyly up at the woman walking beside her. "Thank you for coming to find me…Pam."

Pam smiled down at Callie. "You're welcome."

8

Happily Ever After

Later Callie sat in Andrea's bedroom, surrounded by her books of fairy tales. She still had a hard time thinking of it as her bedroom. But she'd started putting her books on the shelves and that made it feel more like hers. Someone knocked on the door.

"Come in."

Pam peeked in. "Callie, can we talk?"

Callie nodded.

Pam came in and sat down on the side of the bed. "You like fairy tales, don't you?" She reached out and ran a finger across the cover of Snow White.

"Yes."

"Do you think I'm like the wicked stepmothers in them?"

Callie held Hansel and Gretel tight to her chest as she tried to explain. She stared down at the bedspread. Would Pam be mad at her for thinking she was wicked?

"I thought so at first. But then you didn't make me sleep in the attic, even though Andrea didn't want to share her room. And you didn't make me clean out the fireplace." She peered up from under her eyelashes. Pam didn't look mad. "You didn't try to poison me with the broccoli and cheese casserole. And you weren't really trying to lose me in the woods. I mean the city."

Pam's eyes widened. "You thought I was trying to do all that? Oh, Callie, I'm so sorry."

Before Callie could figure out what was happening, Pam reached over and pulled her into a big hug. It smelled of rose perfume. And although it didn't feel quite like her dad's hug, it still felt good. She let her head rest on Pam's shoulder.

Just as the edge of Hansel and Gretel had started to dig into Callie's ribcage, Pam let go. To Callie's surprise, her stepmother had tears in her eyes.

"If I promise not to turn wicked, could we start over?"

Callie grinned.

At that moment a sound came through the open window. It was the sound of a truck's gears.

"Daddy," Callie shouted. She scooted off the bed and ran to the window. "It's Daddy."

"Why don't you run downstairs and say hi to him first," Pam suggested.

Callie thought for a minute. Then she held out her hand. "I think we should go and meet him together. Like a…like a family.

So they did.

The End

About the Author

Susan A. Meyers is the author of several published short stories including "Angie's Homemade Springtime" and "Fairyland." She lives in Oklahoma with her husband, son, and a spoiled cat named Clara. It was Susan's imagination that led her to writing. When her son was little, she'd make up bedtime stories for him. As he grew older, she started writing the stories down. For relaxation Susan loves working puzzles and rooting for the OSU Cowboys. Go Pokes! Susan is a member of the Society of Children's Book Writers and Illustrators (SCBWI). She also belongs to the local critique group, Pennwriters, and the online group, Kidscrit. "Callie and the Stepmother" is Susan's first chapter book.

About the Illustrator

◇◇◇◇◇◇◇◇◇◇◇◇◇◇◇◇◇◇◇◇◇◇◇◇◇◇◇◇◇◇◇◇

Rose Gauss spent all of her extra time as a kid drawing, drawing and climbing a few trees and riding bikes and drawing. She loved colored pencils because they were easy to put-in-your-pocket-and-take-everywhere. But now she works with pen and ink and watercolors and saves the finishing touches for the colored pencils. Rose teaches at several schools a few days a week, working with elementary and middle school-aged children teaching them to draw and paint. She is a member of SCBWI (Society of Children's Book Writers and Illustrators) She and her husband live in an old farmhouse outside of Pittsburgh, Pennsylvania where they raised their three (now grown) children. They have an old tom-cat named D'metri.

Lyranel's Song

Written by Leslie Carmicheal
Illustrated by Elsbet Vance
Ages 8 and up   Grade 3-8   Mid Grade
Hardcover: June $23.95 Special Edition
ISBN 0-9718348-5-7

Trade: July $10.95   ISBN 0-9718348-6-5
LCCN 2005922454

Lyranel has never thought much about Singing. Her mother had been a famous Singer years ago, but she died when Lyranel was still young. Since then, Lyranel's father, the Duke of Trioste, has banned all Singers from his Duchy. The singers that remain Sing their Songs of healing and life in fear and secrecy. When Lyranel wakes her twelfth birthday bursting with Song, she is horrified and tries to hide her new gift from her father. Worse still, a terrible plague threatens her land, especially Singers. Lyranel must learn to come to terms with her new talent. If not, her land and her people just may not survive.

Leslie Carmicheal lives in Canada where she reads, writes and particpates in re-living the Middle Ages. This is her first book for children.

The Gift of Song Can Change All

Angel on My Shoulder

Written by Miriam Hees
Ages 8 and up   Grade 3–8
Type: Christian Mid Grade
Softcover Trade   ISBN: 0-9718348-1-4
LCCN: 2004106683
Price: $5.95

Elizabeth Sinclair works hard at school and even harder at home. Taking care of her younger brother, Jamie is a big job, but she does have an advantage over most girls. Elizabeth has a guardian angel.

When her mother is involved in a tragic accident, Elizabeth is sure life will never be the same again. But the devotion of her best friend, Leslie and her guardian angel, Lily proves to Elizabeth that miracles do happen, even to her.

Join this zany trio as they learn about life, friendship and the power of family love that nothing in *this* world can tear apart.

From Heaven To Earth

Faces in History Book #1
Written by Paula Miller
Illustrated by Chris Forrest
November   Ages 7 and up   Grade 2-5
ISBN 0-9718348-8-1
96 pgs   Chapter Book

The first in the Faces of History Series, this story tells the tale of a boy, Nate, on a cattle ranch in 1880's Montana.

Nate has always wanted a dog, but his Pa hasn't. Only grudgingly does Pa allow Nate to keep the nearly dying puppy he finds. Nate must stuggle to control his new dog and allow the Lord the time to sway Pa's heart.

Paula Miller lives somewhere where she loves to read and write. This is her first book for children. Chris Forrest has been illustrating for many years. This is her first book with Blooming Tree Press.

A Puppy Saves The Day

Angel Eyes

Written by Miriam Hees
Ages 8 and up   Grade 3-8
Type: Christian Mid Grade
Softcover Trade   ISBN: 0-9718348-3-0
LCCN: 2002091744
Price: $5.95

Rachael Miller is trying to make friends, and much to the dismay of her guardian angel, she is trying too hard to fit into the "in crowd".

Turning thirteen is much harder than Rachael expected, especially when she finds herself smack in the middle of the school dance committee, right next to the cutest boy in school!

Be there when Rachael finds out what true friendship means. Laugh and cry with her as she discovers that best friends are hard to find, but angelic ones are even harder to keep.

From Heaven to Earth

Mistletoe Madness

Edited by Miriam Hees
Type: Anthology
Softcover Trade   ISBN: 0-9718348-2-2
LCCN: 2004093501
Price: $8.95

This collection of holiday treats comes to you by way of over thirty authors, poets and illustrators from all over the United States, Canada and Switzerland.

Celebrate this wonderful season with stories such as *First Turkey, Christmas in a Pickle Jar, The Stalking Snowman, Janet's Christmas Candle, Mrs. Whipple's Christmas, Winter Wonderland, The Clauses Go Hollywood* and *Miracle on Stone Street.*

You'll come back again and again to share in these fun, heartwarming and inspiring stories that fill the pages of Mistletoe Madness.

Celebrate The Season

Noises in the Attic

Written by Miriam Hees
Type: Mid Grade
Ages 8 and up   Grade 3–8
Softcover Trade ISBN: 0-9718348-4-9
LCCN: 2003091158
Price: $5.95

Moving to Texas becomes a real adventure when Jilly and Brad Page try to solve a twenty year old mystery.

Flashes of light, bumps in the night and strange noises in the attic force Jilly and Brad to take on a dangerous midnight search for ghosts and timeless treasures.

Join them in their race against time. Be there when they learn about life, friendship and an amazing discovery: Anything is possible — you just have to believe.

Let The Adventure Begin

Ordering Information

Individuals

Although we firmly encourage individuals to buy from their local bookseller, we will fill pre-paid orders received either by mail or through our online store at: www.bloomingtreepress.com.

Bookstores & Wholesalers

We offer all standard trade discounts to booksellers and wholesalers. All of our titles can also be found at: Baker & Taylor.

Libraries/Book Clubs

We offer a discount to any group purchasing more than 8 copies of a single title. Discount depends on quantity ordered. Please email for more information to: email@bloomingtreepress.com.

Selections from Blooming Tree Press

❑ **Callie and the Stepmother** ....0-9718348-0-6—$6.95
❑ **Lyranel's Song** *Hardcover Limited Edition* ....0-9718348-5-7—$23.95
❑ **Lyranel's Song** *Softcover* ....0-9718348-6-5—$10.95
❑ **Angel Eyes**...0-9718348-3-0—$5.95
❑ **Angel on My Shoulder**......................................0-9718348-1-4—$5.95
❑ **One-Eyed Jack** ....0-9718348-8-1—$8.95
❑ **Mistletoe Madness**.. 0-9718348-2-2—$8.95
❑ **Noises in the Attic** .... 0-9718348-4-9—$5.95

For your convenience, Blooming Tree Press accepts Visa, Mastercard, American Express, Discover, Check or Money Order for payment.

Buy them at your local bookstore or use this convenient coupon for ordering.

Blooming Tree Press USA   P.O. Box 140934   Austin, TX 78714-0934

Please send me the Blooming Tree Press Books I have checked above, for which I am enclosing $_____ (please add $5.00 to cover postage and handling). Send check or money order (no cash or C.O.D.'s) or charge my credit card (see limitations above), with a $15 minimum. Prices and numbers are subject to change without notice.

Card# _____ Exp. Date _____
Signature _____
Name _____
Address _____
City _____ State _____ Zip _____
Phone _____

For faster service when ordering by credit card please visit our web site at http://www.bloomingtreepress. com. Allow a minimum of 4-6 weeks for delivery, This offer is subject to change without notice.

www.bloomingtreepress.com